The Creature Coat

To Aaron
J.A.

To my parents, Moe and Va
K.V.

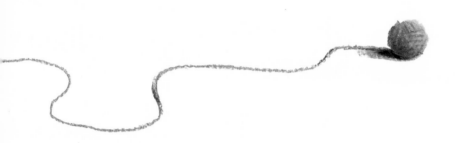

Scholastic Children's Books
Commonwealth House, 1-19 New Oxford Street,
London WC1A 1NU, UK
a division of Scholastic Ltd

London + New York + Toronto + Sydney + Auckland
Mexico City + New Delhi + Hong Kong

First published by Scholastic Press, 2000

Text copyright © Janine Amos 2000
Illustrations copyright © Klaas Verplancke 2000

ISBN 0 590 11161 2

1 3 5 7 9 10 8 6 4 2

Typeset in Truesdell

Printed in China

The rights of Janine Amos and Klaas Verplancke to be identified as
the author and illustrator of this work have been asserted by them
in accordance with the Copyright, Designs and Patents Act, 1988.

The Creature Coat

by
Janine Amos

illustrated by
Klaas Verplancke

Hippo

SCHOLASTIC

Benny's mum was a knitter.
She didn't knit pink fluffy things.
She made magical scarves and mittens,
with wild patterns and colours that
jumped together.

Benny's mum made Benny some gloves
crowded with birds and butterflies.
On windy mornings, Benny could feel
her hands flutter if she held them high.

And once, on a cold, still day, Benny
thought she heard her lion jumper roar.

Benny's mum heard it too.

"I'll knit you a coat," she told Benny.

"A Creature Coat, full of mythical birds and beasts. Think what a noise that will make!"

Benny's mum grabbed up her needles
with a gleam in her eye.
Benny sat on the edge of the chair,
watching. First one sleeve and then
the other came dancing from between
her mum's fingers.

With a stab and a twinkle of silver,
Benny's mum sewed the coat together.
She held it up and Benny put it on.

Unicorns marched down Benny's arms.
Dragons wove their way across her chest.
And on her back sprang a bright
golden bird, with feathers
like darts of rain.

The bird lifted its wings in a terrible shudder. And Benny was carried out of the door, her mum chasing along behind.

"Whee!" laughed Benny's mum in
delight, catching at Benny's hand.
The unicorns threw back their heads
and snorted.

On they all galloped towards the park.
The Creature Coat was beating and
braying with life.

"Look at Benny!" called Benny's friends.
They made a circle and stared.
Benny leapt on to the swing, the
Creature Coat springing and flapping
wildly. Backwards and forwards they
flew in a flash of blue and red and gold.
And the noise! The growls and neighs
and caws and yowls made Benny's
ears tingle.

Then came silence.

The Creature Coat flopped to the ground.

"Hello!" said Benny, trying not to puff.

But Benny's friends wouldn't stay to chat.

"We're late!" they said, eyes on the coat.

"See you another day, Benny."

Benny's mum sighed.

She reached for Benny's hand.

Slowly Benny, her mum and the

Creature Coat made their way home.

But Benny was thinking.

By bedtime Benny was certain.

She looked at the Creature Coat, curled

up on the chair. And she folded her

mum in the warmest of hugs.

"I don't want clothes that stomp and

roar," she whispered.

Understanding, Benny's mum nodded.

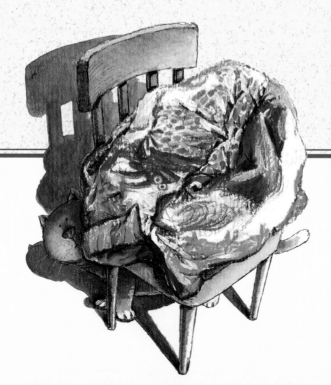

That night Benny's mum gathered up
the Creature Coat. With a stroke and
a pat she settled it into a drawer.
And fastened it tight.

Next day, Benny dressed in quiet clothes
bought from a shop.
At the gate she turned and waved a
Thank You to her mum. Then Benny,
plainly happy, ran to join her friends.

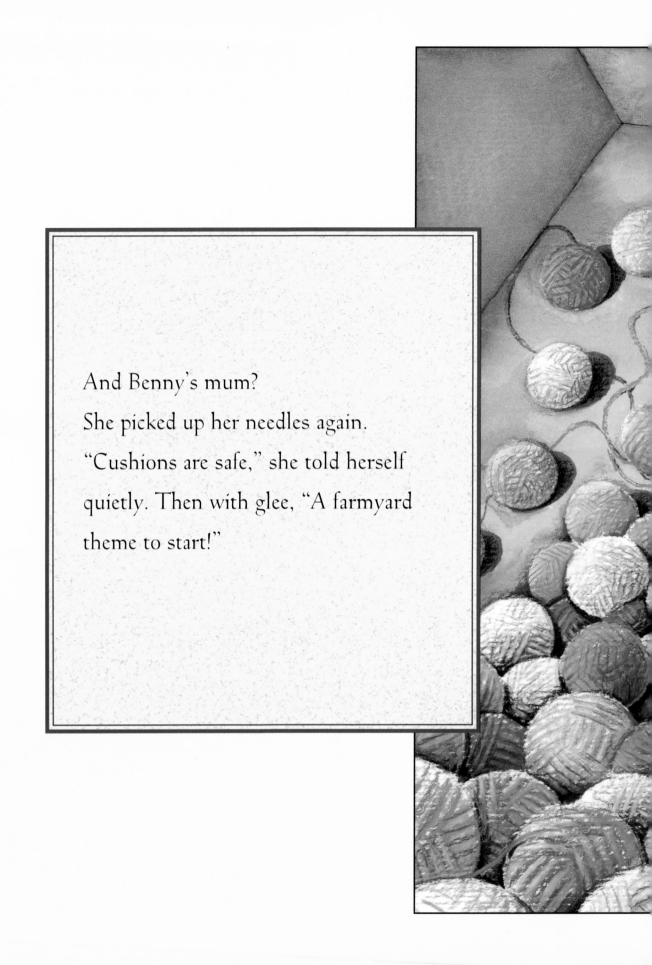

And Benny's mum?

She picked up her needles again.

"Cushions are safe," she told herself

quietly. Then with glee, "A farmyard

theme to start!"

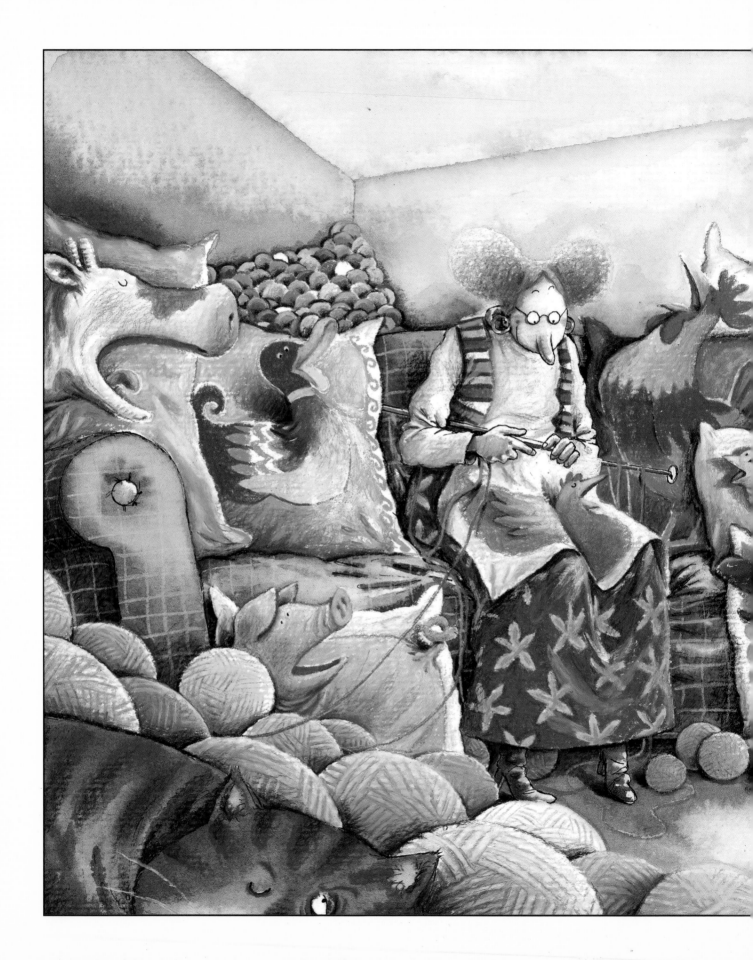

By teatime, a line of cushions marched
across the sofa, patterned with cows
and sheep and hens.
And the room rang with a whole
countryside of sound!